Green Bonds

A Beginner's Guide and an Indian Perspective

Green Bonds

A Beginner's Guide and an Indian Perspective

Pavnesh Kumar
&
Siddhartha Ghosh

ZORBA BOOKS

Published by Zorba Books, April 2022
Website: www.zorbabooks.com
Email: info@zorbabooks.com

Author Name & Copyright © Pavnesh Kumar &
Siddhartha Ghosh
Title :- Green Bonds
Printbook ISBN :- 978-93-93029-71-3
Ebook ISBN :- 978-93-93029-72-0

The publisher under the guidance and direction of the
author has published the contents in this book, and
the publisher takes no responsibility for the contents,
its accuracy, completeness, any inconsistencies, or the
statements made. The contents of the book do not
reflect the opinion of the publisher or the editor. The
publisher and editor shall not be liable for any errors,
omissions, or the reliability of the contents of the book.

Any perceived slight against any person/s, place or
organization is purely unintentional.

Zorba Books Pvt. Ltd. (opc)
Sushant Arcade,
Next to Courtyard Marriot,
Sushant Lok 1, Gurgaon – 122009, India

Printed by Thomson Press (India) Ltd.
B-315, Okhla Industrial Area, Phase 1, New Delhi- 110020

This Book is dedicated to my beloved
Father and Mother.

Their unending encouragement
and blessings are the driving force behind me.
Pavnesh Kumar

In Prayer to the Great Cosmic Energy,
which has guided me for my entire life,
and to whom I reverently refer to as

'The Grand Plan'
Siddhartha Ghosh

Contents

About The Author

Prof. Pavnesh Kumar, is currently working as a Professor and Dean at Pandit Madan Mohan Malaviya School of Commerce and Management Sciences of the Mahatma Gandhi Central University in Bihar, India. He has over 18 years of experience in teaching and conducting research and is the author of numerous books and over 50 research publications. He is a life member of many society and professional organisations, including the Indian Accounting Association, the All India Association for Educational Research, and the Indian Commerce Association, to name a few. He has supervised two Ph.D. scholars and two M.Phil. scholars and has extensive experience in administrative positions such as director, member of the executive council, and chairman of the school board and chairman of the board of postgraduate and undergraduate studies. Additionally, he has attended over 30 international and national seminars. Apart from his work as an Academician and Researcher, he is well-known for his prolific and eloquent speaking, and is frequently invited as a keynote speaker at conferences, webinars, and other literary events. He is currently indulged into research in the fields of international business and finance.

Mr. Siddhartha Ghosh He is a Ph.D. Research Scholar in Department of Management Sciences, Mahatma Gandhi Central University, Bihar and has more than six years of corporate experience having worked in various positions in Academics, Bank, Marketing Research and Skill development. He has authored many articles in various digital mediums and has also written two research papers. His primary areas of interest are Sustainable Finance & International business.

Acknowledgement

To begin, we would like to express our gratitude to **Parampita Parmeshwar**, the All-Mighty God, for providing us with the opportunity to write this book.

We are really thankful of our Honorable Vice Chancellor Prof. Sanjeev Kumar Sharma; he is a true mentor, motivator, and source of inspiration for all of us.

We are also indebted to our Honourable Pro Vice Chancellor Prof. G. Gopal Reddy for continually mentoring us through all stages of this book's completion.

We would like to convey our profound gratitude to everyone who contributed to the composition of this book; without their active cooperation, the book would not have been completed within the set time frame. We are overwhelmed with humility and gratitude to express our admiration to everyone who has assisted us in putting these concepts, which transcend the level of simplicity, into something solid.

Without the help and guidance of parents and friends, no endeavour at any level can be satisfactorily completed. We would like to express our gratitude to our parents for assisting us in obtaining various pieces of information, collecting data, and coaching us from time to time despite their hectic schedules; they provided us with unique ideas for making this book unique.

We offer this book to the very source of information that inspired us

Dr. Pavnesh Kumar
Siddhartha Ghosh

Preface

The time has come for the Financing world as well as the investors to be environmentally conscious.

The financial industry wields great influence when it comes to funding and raising awareness about sustainability issues, whether through enabling for research and development of alternative energy sources or by backing businesses that adhere to fair and sustainable labour practises.

Sustainable finance is described as investment decisions that take into account an economic activity's or project's environmental, social, and governance (ESG) implications.

Environmental factors include climate change mitigation and resource conservation. Human and animal rights, as well as consumer protection and varied hiring practises, are all considered social factors. Governance aspects encompass both public and private enterprises' management, employee relations, and remuneration policies.

Globally, this business models is beginning to shift, as sustainability becomes an increasing necessity for businesses and financial institutions alike.

Consumers want to do business with companies that are socially responsible, and financial organisations are beginning to realize the same. Similarly to how first-generation oil corporations evolved into energy conglomerates as businesses shifted away from carbon-intensive fossil fuels, financial institutions are beginning to see the benefits of sustainable financial practices.

Green Bonds are one of the Investment instruments of Sustainable finance. Green bonds are quickly becoming popular as investors recognize it as a viable investment option for socially responsible businesses. This book discusses Greenbonds in detail covering its global as well as Indianperspective.

1

Concept of Sustainable Finance

Historically, our economy has evolved during periods of abundant natural resources. Business models were built around the exploitation of these natural resources, with less emphasis placed on their conservation. It was in the year 1856, when Scientist Eunice Newton Foote tested the abilities of heat trapping by different gases. She observed in her laboratory that Carbon Dioxide was able to retain heat for a much longer duration when compared with other gases *(Thompson, 2019)*. Her experiments led her to observe that if somehow the

Carbon dioxide content increased in our atmosphere, we can experience higher temperatures just like her experiments.

Her research however was lost to time. It was too early then for humans to fully value the merits and prophetic observation of the research. It was not until 1980s that the scientists observed an increase in temperatures globally. The summer of 1988 was the hottest in the recorded history (of that time) in USA and subsequent years kept on breaking records *(editors, 2021)*. The year also witnessed prevalent droughts and bushfires in the country. The scientists rang the alarm bells and media frenzy insured a wider public attention to the issue. James Hansen (a scientist from NASA) presented before the US Congress saying that global warming was upon the world and he was "99 percent Sure" about it.

Once the ill effects of climate change were evident, efforts were started to mitigate the problem. The year 1992 saw organization of Earth Summit in Brazil's Rio de Janeiro where the participating members concluded that sustainable development could be achieved by transforming private finance *(UNEPFI, 2017)*. The summit was attended by representatives of 13 banks and financial institutions.

The international environmental treaty adopted in Rio, became functional in March 1994 with its objective as "stabilize greenhouse gas concentrations in the atmosphere at a level that would prevent dangerous anthropogenic interference with the climate system" *(UNEPFI, 2017)*.

In September 1994, Geneva, Switzerland hosted the first annual UNEP FI Global Roundtable conference with its topic "Greening Financial Markets". This was followed by the formal adoption of voluntary international standard for corporate environmental management systems; better known as ISO 14001 in 1996. The same year also saw an international conference, the first of its kind on "Implementing Environmental Commitment in the Insurance Industry". This was done with a motive of initiating conversation among leading insurance companies. *(UNEPFI, 2017)*

In December 1997, an international agreement was reached, facilitated by United Nations Framework Convention on Climate Change (UNFCCC) in Kyoto, Japan *(UNEPFI, 2017)*. The agreement committed towards binding the parties to emission reduction targets. In 1999, the Dow Jones launched a global sustainability benchmark, which guided investors for finding profitable companies to invest. These profitable companies however, must follow sustainable business practices. *(UNEPFI, 2017)*

In 2000, Global Reporting Initiative (GRI) was launched. It developed a framework of Sustainability reporting *(UNEPFI, 2017)*. In 2002, the International Conference on Financing for Development was held to find a solution for financing of development in the developing countries. The consensus reached was on resolving the problem of development financing, eradicating poverty and promoting sustainable development. In the same year, a report of UNEP FI was published stressing upon the relevance of climate change problem for the financial services sector. In April 2006, Principles for Responsible Investment (PRI) was launched with signatories from more than 50 countries *(UNEPFI, 2017)*. The works of PRI is consulted by institutional investors for considering Environmental, Social and Governance (ESG) issues into their investments. *(UNEPFI, 2017)*

Regular developments like these finally amalgamated the once distant considered fields of Finance and Sustainability into one. Meanwhile, unchecked resource consumption eventually resulted in widespread carbon emissions, an increase in global temperature, the melting of polar ice caps, and other climate changes. It had become increasingly apparent, at least since 1980s that something needed to be done quickly to halt the process of environmental degradation and to assist in reversing the damage already done; but our reliance on fossil fuels and other non-renewable resources has been a major contributor to the issue of climate change.

It is critical for sustainable development that energy is generated from renewable sources while causing the least amount of damage to the environment. Such initiatives are frequently costly to initiate because they require the use of new technology and alternative energy sources, as well as research and development of a viable model that can be replicated commercially elsewhere.

Any such effort will require significant funding from willing investors to take the risk of investing in such risky ventures. It is critical to remember that no conservation effort can be self-sustaining without adequate financial support. This is where the concept of sustainable finance is applicable.

Sustainable finance is to aid in the implementation of financial decision making while considering the environmental, societal and economical aspects of the prospect. Since last few decades, a strategy has evolved to identify "bad" companies. Here, the term "Bad" has nothing to do with the company but with the type of business it involves into. The concept of societal responsibility comes into picture and companies involved in production of arms and ammunition, tobacco products or gambling are identified. Investment in any such companies is particularly discouraged by banks and financial institutions.

In the coming years, Sustainable finance is expected to evolve into a guiding strategy for investors to invest money while appreciating the long term sustainability prospects of the business; in stark contrast to traditional financial analysis which only cares for better returns while neglecting the environmental consequences.

References

Halley, C. (2019, December 17). How 19th Century Scientists Predicted Global Warming. JSTOR Daily. https://daily.jstor.org/how-19th-century-scientists-predicted-global-warming/

History.com Editors. (2020, November 20). Climate Change History. HISTORY. https://www.history.

com/topics/natural-disasters-and-environment/
history-of-climate-change

The Evolution of Sustainable Finance – United Nations Environment – Finance Initiative. (2019, June 6). UN Environment Programme Finance Initiative. https://www.unepfi.org/news/25th-anniversary/timeline/

2

History of Bonds as a Financial Instrument

Bonds or some financial instrument having similar principles to today's bonds; have been in use from as far back as 2400 BC. *(Cummans et al., 2014)* The excavations at Nippur, Mesopotamia have revealed a stone tablet (currently kept at Museum of Archaeology, Pennsylvania) giving out the first proof of a legally binding bond between two individuals. The discovered stone tablet gave a payment guarantee of grain (common currency of the time period). The discovered bond is a primitive example of 'Surety

Bond' and guaranteed reimbursement in case the principal failed to make the said payment. *(7-Point Timeline of the History of Bonds, 2021)*

Another example of Bonds can be those issued by the administration in Venice (current day Italy). *(Bonds Part VI: An Overview of Medieval Venetian Finance, 2013)* In early years of 1100s they issued these bonds commonly called 'Prestiti' to fund their wars. The Prestiti investors were offered an interest rate of 5% per annum. The bonds market continued to flourish in the region and in 14th century, citizens could buy or trade in these bonds and were offered endless annuity at a given rate. *(Bonds Part VI: An Overview of Medieval Venetian Finance, 2013)*

The first example of government bonds being used comes in 1693 from Bank of England. Here too, the financial instrument was used to fund the ongoing war between England and France *(Milevsky, 2015)*. A same trend is observed in US when government bonds were used in the Revolutionary War (1775-83) to mobilize money to fund the war *(War Bonds, 2021)*. Individuals brought bonds worth more than $27 Million during the time. Similarly, 'Liberty Bonds' were offered in US during First world war at 3.5% interest. The Second World war saw 'Defence

Bonds' which helped the US government to raise $185 Billion in its war efforts. *(War Bonds, 2021)*

How Bonds Work

A bond can be simply understood as a loan; where the purchaser of the Bond pays up money to the issuer of the bond. The money given by the Bond purchaser to the Bond issuer is essentially a loan and interest is applicable on this loan amount known as 'Coupon Rate'. Bond purchasers can be individuals, institutional buyers or other such parties while the bond issuers can be governments, business houses or municipalities. The interest as mentioned in the Coupon Rate is payed by the issuer to the purchaser in mutually accepted time periods which can be semi-annually or annually. The dates at which the interest is payed is called as 'Coupon Dates'.

The bonds 'Face Value' is the amount at which the bond was issued initially by the issuer. Once the Bond reaches its maturity date; the issuer pays this amount back to the bond holder (buyer of the bond). It is worth while to note that while the Face Value of the Bond remained fixed, the actual 'Market Price' of the Bond keeps fluctuating as per the prevalent market conditions. When the Bond's Market price is same as to Its Face Value, the bond is said to be trading 'at par'. If the Market price exceeds the Face value, the bond is said to be trading 'at a premium'; while if the Market price is lower than the Face value the bond is said to be trading 'at a Discount'. Different Bonds compete among themselves in the Bond Market and higher 'Coupon Rate' offering Bonds garner greater demand from the potential Bond buyers. This, in turn affects the fluctuation in the Market Rate of other Bonds.

Types of Bonds in India

- Zero-Coupon Bond – These are usually purchased at a discounted price by the Bond Purchaser. The issuer of such bonds does not pay the interest payments until the Bond reaches its maturity. A amount in Lump sum is paid to the Bondholder at the maturity date.
- Government Security Bonds – These are issued by the Central or State Government as and when there is a need to mobilize funds for any infrastructural or developmental work. These offer a long term investment payment ranging from 5 years to 40 years. The interest rate paid to the Bond holders can be fixed or floating for such type of bonds. While the Central Government Bonds are called as Government Securities (G-Sec); the State Government Bonds are called as State Development

Loans (SDLs).

- Corporate Bonds – These Bonds are issued by companies or corporate houses for mobilizing funds for their business's development. The companies use Bonds when they neither want to take Bank loans; nor willing to offer shares to the public since it dilutes the ownership of the business owners.
- Convertible Bonds – These bonds offer the option to the Bondholders to convert their Bonds into regular shares of the company. By doing so, such bonds offer the advantage of Debt (till remaining in form of Bonds) as well as Equity (once converted into Shares) instruments.
- Inflation Linked Bonds – As the name suggests, these bonds are linked with the inflation index and are issued by the Government. The principal as well as the interest rates keeps on fluctuating, as they are tied with the rate of inflation.
- Sovereign Gold Bonds – These bonds offer the option to the potential Bond buyers to invest in gold while not possessing any in physical form. The interest earned from such a bond is tax-exempted. While individuals can hold 4 Kgs gold worth of such bonds in a financial year; the limit for trusts are fixed at 20 Kgs.
- RBI Floating Rate Saving Bond – These have a maturity period of 7 years with

interest rate varying periodically during the tenure. The interest received under such bonds are taxed according to the tax slab applicable of bondholder's income.

- Bonds offer a low-risk proposal to the investors as it offers a legal binding on the part of the Bond issuer to pay the face value and the interest (as per the decided Coupon Rate) to the Bondholder once maturity date is reached. It also appears a great option for investors to diversify their investment portfolio while reducing risk.

References

Cummans, J., Cussen, M., Cussen, M., Levitt, A., Kranc, J. and Ciura, B., 2014. BondFunds.com. [online] BondFunds.com. Available at: <http://bondfunds.com/education/a-brief-history-of-bond-investing/> [Accessed 7 September 2021].

G. (2018, October 10). 7-Point Timeline of the History of Bonds. GoldenPi | Blogs. https://goldenpi.com/blog/essentials/bond-introduction/7-point-timeline-of-the-history-of-bonds/

L. (2013, December 21). Bonds Part VI: An Overview of Medieval Venetian Finance. Financial Modeling History. https://financialmodelinghistory.wordpress.com/2013/09/08/bonds-part-iv-an-overview-of-medieval-venetian-finance/

A. (2015, August 4). The Earliest Bonds Died With You. FifteenEightyFour | Cambridge University Press. http://www.cambridgeblog.org/2015/05/the-earliest-bonds-died-with-you/

Corporate Finance Institute. (2020, September 15). War Bonds. https://corporatefinanceinstitute.com/resources/knowledge/other/war-bonds/

3

Understanding Green Bonds

Having covered how normal Bonds function as a financial instrument; we will now proceed towards understanding green bonds. A green bond is a specific type of debt security which is issued by governments, corporate businesses or other entities to facilitate mobilizing of capital which can primarily support those infrastructural or developmental projects which have sustainability as their core belief. The motive of the project (i.e. Sustainability) itself is the deciding differentiating factor between a normal bond (having just profit as motive) from a Green bond.

Globally, several developmental banks such as African Development Bank (AfDB), The European Investment Bank (EIB), The World Bank through International Bank for Reconstruction and Development (IBRD) & The International Finance Corporation (IFC), Asian Development Bank (ADB) among many others; have issued green bonds from time to time. The association of Green bonds with such large financial institutions have helped cement the financial instrument's place as a frontrunner to champion the cause of sustainability and catalyse a transformation of 'finance for just profit' to 'finance for the overall betterment'.

China is the largest GB market in terms of issuance between 2012 and 2020. It has issued a whopping 71% of all the GBs globally during this period *(Amundi Asset Management and International Finance Corporation, 2021)*. The corona crisis led to a sharp decrease in GB issuance in India, which slipped from US$ 3.2 Billion in 2019 to US$ 916 Million in 2020. India however, has consistently been next only to China in terms of GBs issuance and has offered GBs worth US$ 10.8 Billion between 2012-20 *(Amundi Asset Management and International Finance Corporation, 2021)*.

The market of GBs slowly expanded and with that; the need for formally identifying the criteria when a said bond can be termed "Green". In 2014, a group of banks came forward to establish the Green Bond Principles (GBP) *(Crédit Agricole, 2014)*. These are a set of guidelines which recognises broad categories; for which bonds can be accepted as green. These include (but not limited to) Sustainable waste management, Sustainable land use, Energy efficiency, Renewable energy, Clean transportation, Biodiversity conservation and Climate change adaptation *(ICMA, 2021)*. Recently, there have been positive developments put into motion with EU's proposed Green Bond Standard (GBS) and European Commission's proposed action plan of Sustainable Finance Disclosure Regulation (SFDR).

Advantages of Green Bonds

Green bonds improves the issuing organisation's reputation and highlights their commitment towards a greener ecosystem. GBs are also instrumental in attracting foreign investors who are ready to invest in such projects. The involvement of foreign investors can reduce the cost of raising the capital for green projects. Since traditional finance just focussed on profits (in a numerical sense), GBs insure finance for eco-friendlier business ventures like renewable energy, waste management, waste recycling etc which can be less lucrative in terms of profits (in numerical sense) but holds the key to long term sustenance of the planet and mankind.

Investors too, are willing to invest in GBs as part of the Corporate Social Responsibility (CSR) initiatives. Investing companies can highlight their contribution and reap benefits of the goodwill thus earned. In many cases, investing in GBs are also encourages by the respective governments in form of Tax exemptions or breaks. All the countries signatory to the Paris Accord tend to give such tax benefits to the investing parties.

Understanding the Emerging Markets of Green Bonds

The emerging green bond markets can be classified regionally as below, along with few (but certainly not limiting to) of its prominent countries:

- East Asia & Pacific consisting of China, Indonesia, Malaysia, the Philippines, Thailand
- Europe & Central Asia consisting of Poland, Hungary
- Latin America and the Caribbean

consisting of Chile, Brazil, Mexico, Panama, Uruguay, Peru and Colombia
- Middle East & North Africa consisting of Egypt, Saudi Arabia and the UAE
- South Asia consisting of India, Bangladesh
- Sub Saharan Africa consisting of South Africa

(Amundi Asset Management and International Finance Corporation, 2021)

Main buyers of Green Bonds

Europe is home to Institutional investors (insurance companies & pension funds) who invest in Green bonds; while USA also has investors having a robust focus on environmental causes. Investors from both Europe and USA were among the first to invest in green bonds. Apart from these two, Japan also has green bond investors. Though, over the period of time, many buyers and institutional investors from other regions are coming forward to commit to the cause of the planet. *(The World Bank & PPIAF, 2017)*

Green Bond Spotlight in 2020

- Green Bonds worth $40 Billion were issued in the emerging markets in 2020 alone.

- A growth of 21% was observed (excluding China) in the emerging markets in 2020 when compared with the previous year.
- A projected issue of $260 billion in green bonds is expected to happen in the emerging markets between 2021-23
- Green bonds have been issued by 43 emerging markets since 2012; with 7 of them making their debut in 2020 alone.

(Amundi Asset Management and International Finance Corporation, 2021)

Challenges for Green Bond

There are few point of concerns for GBs, the primary ones being:

- There have been increased concerns in past few years that projects associated with "Green" ventures are not as green as they claim to be. Sometimes, funds amassed from green bonds go towards projects, which claim to be "sustainable" just on paper but have no tangible results on the ground. Worse scenarios may see funds diverted towards harming the environment (like regular business ventures).
- In India, a general lack of verifiable credit rating or guidelines for GBs is a major problem.
- Specifically, in the case of India; GBs have a less awareness level when compared globally. (RBI, 2021)

References

Amundi Asset Management and International Finance Corporation. (2021). Emerging Market Green Bonds Report 2020. Amundi and IFC. https://www.ifc.org/wps/wcm/connect/0fab2dcd-25c9-48cd-b9a8-d6cc4901066e/2021.04+-+Emerging+Market+Green+Bonds+Report+2020+-+EN.pdf?MOD=AJPERES&CVID=nBW.6AT

Crédit Agricole. (2014). Joint press release. https://www.ca-cib.com/sites/default/files/2017-03/2014-01-13-cp-cacib-green-bond-principles-en-final.pdf

ICMA. (2021, June). ICMA's Green Bond Principles. https://www.icmagroup.org/assets/documents/Sustainable-finance/2021-updates/Green-Bond-Principles-June-2021-140621.pdf

The World Bank & PPIAF. (2017). What are Green Bonds. https://documents1.worldbank.org/curated/en/400251468187810398/pdf/99662-REVISED-WB-Green-Bond-Box393208B-PUBLIC.pdf

RBI.(2021,January). Green Finance in India: Progress and Challenges (RBI Bulletin). January 2021.https://rbidocs.rbi.org.in/rdocs/Bulletin/PDFs/04AR_2101202185D9B6905ADD465CB7DD280B88266F77.PDF

4

Types of Green Bonds and its Uses across Various Sectors

Types of Green Bonds

Green bonds can be categorised as below:

- "Use of Proceeds" GB – In financial terms, Proceeds denotes the money which has been brought in through some transaction or event. The money brought by these type of GBs are set apart specifically for a Green project. Credit ratings of such GBs tend to remain same with other bonds offered by the issuing institution.
- "Use of Proceeds" Revenue Bond – Proceeds from such bonds are earmarked for

backing or refinancing purposes of ongoing green projects. The bondholders have the flexibility to get coupon payments through revenue generated by issuing institution through subscription fees of products/services or other relevant sources.

- Project GB – Proceeds from such GBs are 'Ring Fenced' i.e. having specific restriction to be used in initiation or functioning of a particular green project. The bondholders enjoy the privilege to be extended payments (in case of default) through the liquidation of project's assets and balance sheet.

- Securitisation Bond – Funds mobilized through such GBs are utilized for refinancing portfolios of green projects. In this case, the portfolios of green project are formed in a group (i.e. portfolio) and the bondholders have the right to be made coupon payments or lump sum payments through such green projects bunched together.

- Covered GB – These are issued by banks or other such institutions who borrow against a collateral of a pool of assets. The proceeds coming from such bonds can only be used for those green projects which are included in the pre-identified pool of assets. In case, the bond issuer is unable to repay; the bondholders can demand payments to be made by liquidating a part or whole of the pool of assets.

- Other debt instruments – Apart from the types mentioned above, there can be other debt instrument which can qualify as GB in various scenarios. These may included convertible GBs (which can be converted into normal stocks by the bondholders if they wish so), commercial papers and Debentures.
- *(McKenzie, 2019)*

Uses across Various Sectors

- Solar Energy – Solar energy sector is one of the prominent sector where green bonds are used to either initiate new projects or refinancing ongoing projects. Green bonds are not only used for solar energy generation projects; but transmission and other supporting infrastructure as well. Solar hot water systems and other thermal facilities also make use of GBs for financing purposes. Solar energy is expected to play a pivotal role in producing clean electricity and is expected to contribute around 22% or the world's electricity supply by 2050.
- Wind Energy – Wind energy in as another avenue where GBs are used. It is used to fund wind energy generation facilities along with transmission facilities like grid connections, transformers, equipment storage, support vehicles etc. GBs can also be used for distribution components like wind turbines and platforms.
- Green Buildings – Building construction

might seem of a lesser culprit in carbon emissions on the surface; but according to experts contribute to 40% of carbon emissions globally. The building construction sector is well behind the required carbon cuts from its processes to ensure towards efforts to curb global temperature rise to 2° Celsius as committed in Paris Climate agreement of 2015. A lifetime carbon assessment of the construction project is done. Along with this, the building is designed in a way to use reduced operational energy over its lifetime. Also, raw materials sourced for building construction is modified wherever possible to reduce carbon production while transportation process of the raw materials. GBs are used for constructing Low Carbon buildings or projects, which comply with three components of Mitigation, Adaptation and Disclosure.

- Transportation – A large part of global human population use some sort of transportation daily to commute to their work places, markets, schools, colleges, places of worship or other such avenues. It is estimated that the transport sector alone (including air, land and sea mediums) contributes to 23% of global energy-related CO_2 emissions. With the rise in global population, use of transportation is expected to increase and with that; an increase in carbon emissions. Newer transport mediums based on electricity, Hydrogen or other Zero-direct emission fuels are being tested. Also, infrastructure for public transportation like cycling paths, public walking ways and even Bus Rapid Transport (BRT) Systems are being encouraged in bigger cities. However, since real estate has a cost involved with it and construction as well is not cheap; hence GBs are used to fund infrastructural projects of transportation.

- Agribusiness & Forestry – With the world population expected to reach to 10 billion individuals by 2050, it is expected that food demand will shoot up more than 50% with global grain demand to increase two-folds. Chemical pesticides and fertilizers can only increase the crop yield to a limit with harmful effects on the soil. There has been increasing calls to revolutionize the agricultural land use along with modifying the supply chain to a "Zero Deforestation Supply Chain". Climate change is also an issue looming large to mitigate in the near future. GBs are used for development of crop yield increasing technologies with no side effects on the land of the nutritional content of the crop itself.

- Industrial Efficiency – Industries are one of the biggest contributor in carbon emissions and hence have huge potential to transform their production process to ensure minimum to log damage on the eco-system. The carbon emissions can be considered and mitigated at each stage of value chain right from procuring raw materials from less carbon intensive sources, to using greener mediums of transportation, using less carbon intensive way or production and finally tweaking the packaging to eco-friendlier options. Improving industrial efficiency requires research apart from modifying the production process at every step. GBs are used to mobilize funds for such industrial projects.

- Bioenergy – Bioenergy is the energy produced from processing solids, liquids or gases derived from biomass. Biomass is renewable organic matter sourced from plants & animals, like dried leaves, agricultural waste, wood etc. Biomass can also be sourced from organic wastes produced during industrial activity. Processing of Biomass yields two distinct substances; viz. Biofuel and Biogas. Biofuel is a liquid made by fermenting carbohydrate rich biomass. It contains high amount of ethanol. Biogas is fuel in gas form and is a mixture of Carbon Dioxide (CO_2) and Methane (CH_4). It is produced when organic matter is broken down due to bacterial activity. GBs are used for energy projects in areas where agriculture or livestock is the primary occupation since it supplies enough organic matter to sustain the project.

- Other areas where GBs are used to initiate of refinance infrastructural projects include Electrical grids & storage, Geothermal energy, Hydropower, Land conservation & Restoration, Marine Renewable energy, Shipping and other such projects having the motive of reducing carbon emissions in totality

.(Initiative, 2021)

References

McKenzie, B., 2019. Green Bonds – An Overview. [online] Bakermckenzie.com. Available at: <https://www.bakermckenzie.com/en/-/media/files/insight/publications/2019/05/green-bonds--an-overview--may-2019.pdf> [Accessed 8 September 2021].

Initiative, C., 2021. Sector Criteria Available for Certification. [online] Climate Bonds Initiative. Available at: <https://www.climatebonds.net/standard/available> [Accessed 8 September 2021].

5

Private Sector Green Bond Issuance in India

India has adopted the GBs swiftly with SEBI's directives firmly in place. Bombay stock exchange has launched India International Exchange Limited (India INX) on January 2017. India INX has introduced the Global Securities Market platform, offering a transparent and efficient method to raise capital. The platform offers a debt-listing framework at par with international listing venues like London, Singapore or Luxembourg. Subsequent chapters will go into detail on Indian GB framework, guidelines and legalities. In this chapter however, we will be discussing few of the major green bond offerings of private business entities.

- Adani Electricity Mumbai Limited – AEML incepted in 1926 and is involved in supplying electricity in Mumbai and its suburbs. It serves to around 67% of the population and covers approximately 85% of its geographical area. Apart from Mumbai, it also serves in the Thane District and the Mira-Bhayander Municipal area *(Electricity, 2021)(pg.3)*. AEML issued Sustainability-Linked Bonds (SLBs). SLBs have a key sustainability-linked feature, which provides the bondholder with a one-time adjustment (+0.15% increase per annum) in the rate of interest offered in case the bond issuer (AEML in this case) fails to achieve their pre-set Sustainability Performance Targets (SPTs). A second failure in reaching the SPT by the second Target Observation Date will result in an another increase of 0.15% interest for the bondholder *(Electricity, 2021)(pg.14)*. US $300,000,000 worth of green bonds were issued by AEML for an offered interest rate of 3.867% and due for maturity after a 10 year period reaching in 2031 *(Exchange, 2021)*.
- Adani Green Energy UP Ltd – AGEL is one of the largest companies in India functioning in renewable energy sector. The company into development, building,

operating, owning and maintaining utility-scale grid-connected renewable energy projects and has an energy creation portfolio of 13,990 MW *(Energy Ltd, 2021)*. The company works in Solar energy & wind energy. The company has 51 Solar power plants commissioned with some of them located in Kamuthi (TN), Pavagada (Karnataka), Bathinda (Punjab) and Durg (Chattisgarh). The company also has 6 wind power generation stations commissioned in Madhya Pradesh and Gujrat *(Energy Ltd, 2021)*. US $500,000,000 worth of Senior secured notes were issued by AGEL for an offered interest rate of 6.25% and due for maturity in 2024 *(Exchange, 2021)*.

- ReNew Wind Energy Delhi Private Limited (along with 9 other group companies) ~ ReNew Power was founded in 2011 by Mr. Sumant Sinha. The company is a subsidiary of ReNew Energy Global PLC and is one of the largest renewable energy company in India in terms of total energy generation capacity. The company caters to both commercial and industrial customers with its utility scale solar & wind energy projects; along with distributed solar energy projects *(Power, 2021)*. The company is backed by global investors few of them being Goldman Sachs, Global environment fund and Abu Dhabi Investment authority *(Power, 2021)*. In 2020 alone,

ReNew raised US$ 1045 Million through overseas sale of green bonds. Bonds worth US $585,000,000 were sold twice at 4.5% Coupon rate and are due for maturity in 2028 *(Exchange, 2021)*.

- JSW Hydro Energy Limited ~ JSW Energy limited is a part of JSW Group having presence in infrastructure, cement, steel production and Energy sector. JSW Energy has thermal, hydro and Solar power plants *(Energy Plants, 2021)*. JSW Hydro Energy Limited (JSWHEL) was born in September 2015 with the acquisition of Jaiprakash Power Ventures Limited. JSWHEL owns hydroelectric power plants located on Sutlej river in Karcham and Baspa in Himachal Pradesh *(Hydro Energy, 2021) (Pg.2)*. The group has also incorporated a 100% own subsidiary JSW Energy (Kutehr) Limited for setting up a 240 MW hydroelectric power plant in the Ravi basin of Chamba district in Himachal Pradesh. JSWHEL in May 2021 debuted with its green bond worth US $ 707 Million. The bond issue was subscribed 4x times and offered a coupon rate of 4.125% with a 10 Year maturity period *(Roy, 2021)*.
- CLP India Pvt. Limited ~ CLP India is a subsidiary of CLP Group. CLP India has maintained a presence in Indian markets from 2002 when it acquired a 655 MW gas-fired power station in Bharuch, Gujarat

(Limited, 2021). Since then, the company has built a 3000 MW diversified energy portfolio in the country. It owns wind energy projects, solar energy projects, combined cycle power plants and power transmission projects. The company raised US $ 90 Million through issuance of green bonds in September 2015. The bonds had an AA rating (considered very safe) and offered an attractive coupon rate of 9.15% per annum. The proceeds from the bond issuance were utilised for setting up new renewable energy spaces in India *(Prasad, 2021).*

- Tata Cleantech Capital Limited – TCCL was formed as a joint venture between Tata Capital Limited and the International Finance Corporation in 2011 *(Capital, 2021).* It is the first financial institution of Private sector in India that is solely focussed on Green finance and aims to offer business solutions including advisory and debt capital services for clean technology and infrastructure space. It is a 'non-deposit accepting' non-banking finance company (NBFC) approved by Reserve Bank of India. The NBFC extends commercial lending to businesses operating in the space of energy production from renewable sources like wind & solar, waste management, water management and energy efficiency. The company is rated 'AAA' by CRISIL and is the only Indian company to be recognised as "Green Bank" *(Capital, 2021).* In January 2019, TCCL raised Rupees 180 Crores through sale of GBs having a maturity date after 5 years. The bonds were sold to Netherlands based development bank FMO (Financierings-Maatschappij voor Ontwikkelingslanden N.V) *(Times, 2021).* The proceeds from the bond issuance are to be used for 2 solar power projects having the capacity of 220 MW and 57.5 MW located in Karnataka and Telangana respectively

- Azure Power Global Limited ~ APG limited was founded in 2008 and aims for providing affordable solar power. The company has developed solar projects in Punjab, Gujarat, Rajasthan, Chhattisgarh and Jharkhand. As of 2020, APG has more than 7 GW power portfolio across India *(Power, 2021).* In August 2021, the company announced issuance of dollar green bond to the tune of US $ 414 Million. The bonds have a 5 Year maturity period and were issued at a Coupon rate of 3.575%. This bond issuance is the lowest ever yield for any renewable energy company in India. The proceeds from the bond issuance is to be used for refinancing the existing green bonds issued in 2017 and due for maturity in 2022 (with a 5.5% Coupon rate) *(Power, 2021).*

- The above instances are not the only Green bond issuance but a few from the many. With India's strong political commitment to address the climate issue; coupled with good progress made so far in achieving Paris Agreement's established Nationally Determined Contributions (NDCs), the future will certainly see many more GB issuance.

References

Electricity, A. (2021). Sustainability-Linked Bond Framework Adani Electricity Mumbai Limited July 2021. Adanielectricity. com. Retrieved 8 September 2021, from https://www.adanielectricity.com/-/media/ 1373961AC8F94C2A9502BC50AAA7DB0E. ashx?h=16&thn=1&w=16.

Exchange, I. (2021). India Inx-India International Exchange IFSC Ltd, GIFT City, SEZ. Indiainx.com. Retrieved 8 September 2021, from https://www. indiainx.com/static/gssustainablebonds.aspx.

Energy Ltd, A. (2021). Adani Green Energy Ltd. Adanigreenenergy.com. Retrieved 8 September 2021, from https://www.adanigreenenergy.com/ about-us.

Power, R. (2021). Homepage. Renew Power. Retrieved 8 September 2021, from https://renewpower.in/.

Power, R. (2021). Our Partners. Renew Power. Retrieved 8 September 2021, from https://renewpower.in/about-us/our-partners/.

Energy Plants, J. (2021). JSW - JSW Energy Plants. Jsw.in. Retrieved 8 September 2021, from https://www.jsw.in/energy/jsw-energy-plants-0.

Roy, A. (2021). JSW Hydro Energy raises $707 million in debut 10-year green bond issue. Business-standard.com. Retrieved 8 September 2021, from https://www.business-standard.com/article/companies/jsw-hydro-energy-raises-750-million-in-debut-10-year-green-bond-issue-121051001268_1.html.

Hydro Energy, J. (2021). JSW Hydro Energy Green Bond Framework. Jsw.in. Retrieved 8 September 2021, from https://www.jsw.in/sites/default/files/assets/industry/energy/IR/JSW%20Energy%20Investor%20Presentation/JSW%20Hydro%20Energy-Green%20Bond%20Framework%20May%202021.PDF.

Limited, C. (2021). CLP India Private Limited. Clpindia.in. Retrieved 8 September 2021, from https://www.clpindia.in/history.html.

Prasad, R. (2021). CLP India's wind energy arm raises around Rs 300 crore via green bonds. The Economic Times. Retrieved 8 September 2021, from https://economictimes.indiatimes.com/markets/bonds/clp-indias-wind-energy-arm-raises-around-rs-300-crore-via-green-bonds/articleshow/78655071.cms.

Capital, T. (2021). Tata Cleantech Capital - Initiating Climate Finances with Innovative Solutions. Tatacapital.com. Retrieved 8 September 2021, from https://www.tatacapital.com/tccl.html.

Times, T. (2021). Tata Cleantech Capital raises Rs 180 crore via maiden green bond. The Economic Times. Retrieved 8 September 2021, from https://m.economictimes.com/markets/stocks/news/tata-cleantech-capital-raises-rs-180-crore-via-maiden-green-bond/articleshow/67348309.cms.

Power, A. (2021). Solar Energy Electricity | Solar Power Project | Renewable Energy. Azurepower.com. Retrieved 8 September 2021, from https://www.azurepower.com/about-us.

Power, A. (2021). US$414 Million Green Bond Issuance at Lowest Ever Yield for Renewable

Energy Company in India. Investors.azurepower. com. Retrieved 8 September 2021, from http://investors.azurepower.com/press-releas es/2021/08-12-2021-145021082.

6

Public Sector Green Bond Issuance in India

In the earlier chapter, we have seen how Private businesses in India have used GBs to raise capital for the Green projects. However, they are not certainly not alone in the Green bond rush. The Public Sector too has welcomed GBs with open arms and have used it to mobilize fund from overseas. GBs serve as a great instrument for foreign institutional and individual investors willing to invest in an environmentally responsible green business project.

Below mentioned are few of such Public sector GB issuances:

- Indian Railway Finance Corporation Limited – IRFC was set up on 12 December 1986 as a dedicated financing arm devoted for raising funds from domestic and international capital markets for the development of Indian railways. It is a Schedule 'A' Public sector enterprise and has played a pivotal part in last 30 years for the expansion and sustenance of not just Indian railways but other Railway entities like Konkan Railway Corporation Limited (KRCL), Rail Vikas Nigam Limited (RVNL), Railtel etc. The funding from IRFC helped the acquisition of more than 70% of total rolling stock fleet, which included railway locomotives, passenger coaches and wagons *(Corporation, 2021)*. It holds the highest Credit rating of AAA by CRISIL, CARE and ICRA credit rating agencies. US $ 500,000,000 worth of Notes were issued by IRFC with an offered coupon rate of 3.835% and will be due for maturity in 2027 *(Exchange, 2021)*.
- State Bank of India – SBI is the largest public sector bank in India and has issued green bonds from time to time. In March 2020, it raised US $100 million in green bonds. The bank planned to issue the bonds through its London branch and intended to list them on Singapore Exchange (SGX).

This was the bank's third issue of green bonds having already raised US $ 700 Million from previous two attempts *(Ghosh, 2021)*. It had also issued Floating rate notes worth US$ 100,000,000 using India INX's Global Securities Market platform due to mature in 2022. On a separate occasion, the same platform was used to issue notes worth US$ 650,000,000 at 4.5% coupon rate with a maturity date in 2023 *(Exchange, 2021)*.

- NTPC Limited ~ The National Thermal Power Commission Limited was established in 1975 and is the largest energy conglomerate in India. The company traditionally relied on fossil fuels for energy production but has since ventured in generating power from hydro plants, nuclear plants and other renewable sources. The company has also diversified in consultancy, training of human resource, rural electrification and ash utilisation. The company owns 1 Hydro, 1 Wind, 13 Solar, 1 small hydro and 7 gas based power generation plants. Under Joint Venture, the company has 4 gas based and 13 renewable energy projects *("NTPC Overview | NTPC", 2021)*. In August 2016, the company raised US $ 300 Million by Green masala bonds, which were listed in London Stock Exchange. The annual coupon rate offered to overseas investors was a staggering 7.48%

(Exchange, 2021). The company has a long-term goal of generating nearly 28% of its energy production from renewable sources by 2032 and the proceeds from the bond issuance was reported to be planned for utilisation towards solar power projects *("India's NTPC Raises $300 Million In Green Bonds Issue", 2016)*

- EXIM Bank ~ Exim Bank was formed in 1982, to serve as a pioneering institution for economic growth by eliminating constraints like inadequate infrastructure. The bak received vital support from Ministry of Commerce, Govt. of India and regularly emphasised on export promotion. The institution today serves as to businesses for import of technology from abroad, product development for export, export marketing, pre & post shipping and investment in overseas *(Bank, 2021)*. In March 2015, the bank raised US $ 500 million by Green bond issuance for 5 years period. The coupon rate offered was 2.75% and the issue was oversubscribed more than three times. The proceeds from the bond issuance was planned for utilization in eligible green projects in not only India but Sri Lanka and Bangladesh as well *(Bureau, 2015)*.
- Rural Electrification Corporation Limited - REC functions under the guidance from Ministry of Power (Govt. of India) and is a Navratna company. It was estab-

lished in 1969, at a time of severe droughts, to strengthen the Agricultural economy of India by facilitating irrigation through pump-sets; rather than dependency on monsoons. The company later started extending financial loans (both Short & Medium term) in power sector for business entities into generation, transmission or distribution of power *(Ltd., 2021)*. REC Limited offered its first Green bond in June 2017 and raised US $ 450 Million from the proceeds. It was a 10 Year maturity period bond and offered a coupon rate of 3.965%. The bond was listed in London's International Security Market (ISM) and was oversubscribed by 3.9 times. The proceeds were expected to play a pivotal role in financing green power generation projects so as to meet the Central Government's target of producing 175GW of electricity from renewable resources by 2022 *(International, 2017)*.

- Ghaziabad Municipal Corporation ~ The GMC civic body in Uttar Pradesh became India's first municipal corporation in April 2021; to successfully list its Green Municipal Bonds in Bombay Stock Exchange. The proceeds from the bonds were announced to raise Rupees 150 Crores at a Coupon rate of 8.1% per annum *(Writer, 2021)*. The union government gave a 19.5 crore incentive to GMC for raising funds through municipal bonds. The green bonds were rated 'AA' by both India Ratings and Brickworks and has a maturity period of 10 years. The mobilized money is expected to be used for establishing a network of pipes supplying water through water meters; and a tertiary water treatment plant in the city *(Moneycontrol, 2021).*

With Green bonds being increasingly used by PSUs successfully in attracting investors from overseas, it is likely that we will see many more such GB offerings from them in the future as well.

References

Corporation, I. (2021). Company Profile. irfc.nic.in. Retrieved 8 September 2021, from https://irfc.nic.in/company-profile/.

Exchange, I. (2021). India Inx-India International Exchange IFSC Ltd, GIFT City, SEZ. Indiainx.com. Retrieved 8 September 2021, from https://www.indiainx.com/static/gssustainablebonds.aspx.

Ghosh, S. (2021). State Bank of India raises $100 million in green bonds. mint. Retrieved 8 September 2021, from https://www.livemint.com/companies/news/state-bank-of-india-raises-100-million-in-green-bonds-11585408209737.html.

Exchange, L. (2021). NTPC lists world's first green Masala bond by an Indian issuer on London Stock Exchange. London Stock Exchange. Retrieved 8 September 2021, from https://www.londonstockexchange.com/discover/news-and-insights/ntpc-lists-worlds-first-green-masala-bond-indian-issuer-london-stock-exchange.

Standard, B. (2021). NTPC declares its Energy Compact Goals for sustainability at UN dialogue. Business-standard.com. Retrieved 8 September 2021, from https://www.business-standard.com/article/companies/ntpc-declares-its-energy-compact-goals-for-sustainability-at-un-dialogue-121062800064_1.html.

India's NTPC Raises $300 Million In Green Bonds Issue. CleanTechnica. (2016). Retrieved 8 September 2021, from https://cleantechnica.com/2016/08/08/indias-ntpc-raises-300-million-green-bonds-issue/.

Bureau, B. (2015). Exim Bank green bond issue raises $500 mn. @businessline. Retrieved 8 September 2021, from https://www.thehindubusinessline.com/markets/exim-bank-green-bond-issue-raises-500-mn/article7032109.ece.

Ltd., R. (2021). REC LTD - Corporate Profile. Recindia.nic.in. Retrieved 8 September 2021, from https://www.recindia.nic.in/corporate-profile.

International, A. (2017). Rural Electrification Corporation of India launches first Green Bond in London. ANI News. Retrieved 8 September 2021, from https://www.aninews.in/news/business/rural-electrification-corporation-of-india-launches-first-green-bond-in-london/.

Moneycontrol, M. (2021). India's First Rs 150 Crore Ghaziabad Green Bond Lists On The BSE Bond Platform. Moneycontrol. Retrieved 8 September 2021, from https://www.moneycontrol.com/news/business/real-estate/indias-first-rs-150-crore-ghaziabad-green-bond-lists-on-the-bse-bond-platform-6744511.html.

Writer, S. (2021). Ghaziabad Municipal Corporation' green bond listed on BSE bond platform. mint. Retrieved 8 September 2021, from https://www.livemint.com/news/india/ghaziabad-municipal-corporation-green-bond-listed-on-bse-bond-platform-11617874266775.html.

7

Global Green Bond Exchanges

Green bonds had a humble beginning but have since grown massively in size. The GB market was worth US $ 3 billion in 2012, which increased more than 25 time to US $ 81 Billion until 2016 *(Climate Bonds Initiative, 2017)*. This phenomenal growth not only attracted governments, corporates and investors but, a need for a separate dedicated exchange committed to dealing in Green bonds or other such green investments was felt.

Once potential investment options (all green-sustainable in nature) are listed in one place i.e.

exchange; it becomes easier for the investors to peruse the investment option while also comparing it to other available alternatives to take a well formed decision. The exchange also serves the bond issuers with a large potential investor base; having institutional investors like mutual fund houses, insurance companies, pension funds, other willing institutions and individual investors as well.

In addition, green bonds exchange only serve sustainable investment options in their listing. The exchange cuts on time and transaction costs otherwise required for a potential GB issuer or seller to meet and finalize the selling of the investment instrument. Hence, such exchanges also improve the liquidity of GBs and other such investments. Lastly, such exchanges have stringent rules of GB listing which ensures that the bond issuers follow all the necessary good practices. Such elaborate and tight listing process ensures greater Green bond transparency and promotes it as a viable investment alternative with an environmental betterment motive.

Examples of Green Bond Exchanges or Dedicated Segments

The green bonds either can have their own full-fledged bond exchange, or can have a dedicated segment in the prominent stock exchanges. We will be going through few of such specialised Green Bond marketplaces in this section.

- Luxembourg Green Exchange (LGX) – LGX was established in 2016 and is a global leading dedicated platform for dealing in green, sustainable and social securities. It was the world's first exchange of its kind to be fully devoted to the cause of sustainability. The exchange maintains a presence of 135 international issuers hailing from 32 countries. The exchange is capable of issuing securities in 32 different currencies and as of 31st August 2020, displayed 796 green, sustainable and social securities in its list worth US $ 356 billion. The exchange follows bond standards as prescribed in Sustainability-Linked Bond Principles (SLBP) and Sustainability Bond Guidelines (SBG), Social Bond Principles (SBP), ASEAN Green Bond Standards and other such frameworks. It follows various labels for the bond listings such as LuxFLAG Climate Finance, Social, Environment and ESG, the French established TEEC and SRI, the Nordic Swan Ecolabel and Austrian ecolabel for securities; to name a few. *(Climate Change, 2021)*
- Global Securities Market Platform (India INX) – The Bombay Stock Exchange (BSE) launched its wholly owned subsidiary 'India INX' on 9th January 2017. The

newly formed exchange was inaugurated by Hon'ble Prime Minister, Shri Narendra Modi and commenced its operations from 16*th* January 2017. India INX launched the Global Securities Market Platform, which offers a debt-listing platform at par with international markets like Luxembourg, Singapore, and London etc. The Global Securities Market is a specialised segment dealing in Green and sustainable investments and has issued bonds worth more than US $ 28 million from 72 issuers. Adani Green Energy Limited's bonds worth US $ 500 Million were the first to be listed in the exclusive green listing and trading ePlatform. *(INX, 2021)*

- It has helped companies like SBI, EXIM bank, NTPC, Adani Port, Rural Electrification Corp. and Asian Development Bank to list their offering on the state of art platform. The Global Securities Market aims to provide a comprehensive range of securities sourced from a wide spectrum of issuers; while also maintaining the international listing standards, regulatory practices, competitive pricing and settlement of securities. *(INX, 2021)*

- Nasdaq Sustainable Bond Network (NSBN) – In 2015 the 'National Association of Securities Dealers Automated Quotations' commonly known as NASDAQ launched the Nasdaq Sustainable Debt

Market (NSDM). It served as a common platform for listing GBs and other such financial instruments dedicated to promote sustainability *(Exchange Initiative, 2021).* Amidst Corona pandemic in 2020, the NSDM registered an increase in listed volumes chiefly attributed to fundraising efforts from various governments, organisations and NGOs.

- In June 2021, The Nasdaq Sustainable Bond network (NSBN) was launched. It can be seen an extension of the Nasdaq Sustainable Debt Market and is dedicated to sustainable securities like Luxembourg Green Exchange. Through this global platform, investors are expected to get access to more than 6,500 bonds being issued by 600 issuers hailing from 51 countries. The newly launched electrinoc platform operates under the set guidelines of the International Capital Markets Association (ICMA). *(Kerencheva, 2021)*

Apart from the above discussed examples, there are a number of Green and Sustainable Bond dedicated sections in various international stock exchanges (SE) like Oslo SE, Stockholm SE, London SE, Shanghai SE, Mexico SE, Taipei exchange, Johannesburg SE, Vienna exchange, Swiss SE, Frankfurt SE, Santiago SE, Brazil SE, Nigerian SE, Toronto SE, Singapore SE etc.

References

Climate Bonds Initiative. (2017). The role of exchanges in accelerating the growth of the green bond market (p. 2). Climate Bonds Initiative. Retrieved from https://www.climatebonds.net/files/files/RoleStock%20Exchanges.pdf

Exchange, L. (2021). Green bonds. Bourse.lu. Retrieved 8 September 2021, from https://www.bourse.lu/green-bonds.

Climate Change, U. (2021). The Luxembourg Green Exchange | Luxembourg. Unfccc.int. Retrieved 8 September 2021, from https://unfccc.int/climate-action/momentum-for-change/financing-for-climate-friendly-investment/luxembourg-green-exchange.

INX, I. (2021). India Inx-India International Exchange IFSC Ltd, GIFT City, SEZ. Indiainx.com. Retrieved 8 September 2021, from https://www.indiainx.com/static/about.aspx.

Kerencheva, E. (2021). Nasdaq Launches Sustainable Bond Investor Portal - ESG Today. ESG Today. Retrieved 8 September 2021, from https://www.esgtoday.com/nasdaq-launches-sustainable-bond-investor-portal/.

Exchange Initiative, S. (2021). Exchange in Focus: Nasdaq Sustainable Bond Network Builds a Framework for a Sustainable Future | Sustainable Stock Exchanges. Sseinitiative.org. Retrieved 8 September 2021, from https://sseinitiative.org/all-news/exchange-in-focus-nasdaq-sustainable-bond-network-builds-a-framework-for-a-sustainable-future/.

BBVA, B. (2021). BBVA, the first Spanish bank on the Nasdaq sustainable debt market. NEWS BBVA. Retrieved 8 September 2021, from https://www.bbva.com/en/bbva-the-first-spanish-bank-on-the-nasdaq-sustainable-debt-market/.

8

Different Sustainable Bond Standards

Necessity of Sustainable Bond Standards

We have covered in the previous chapters how sustainable bonds have developed from just an idea to an actual financial instrument dedicated to championing the cause of sustainability. The international market of sustainable bonds have expanded rapidly in last few years and a similar trend is expected to follow with more and more people becoming aware about this viable investment option.

With the rapid rise of sustainable bonds, a number of sustainable green bonds markets or dedicated segment in established stock exchanges have sprung up. While such bond markets or segments are responsible to list qualifying Green or sustainable bonds for attracting attention of the investors, they cannot establish the authenticity of such bonds on their own. Hence, there is an underlying need to set some standards, which a bond must meet to qualify itself as a "Green Bond" or "Sustainable Bond". This will also prevent regular bonds to masquerade as these, and thus cementing the reputation of such bonds without any doubts.

Some established Sustainable Bond Standards

International Capital Market Association (ICMA) – ICMA traces its origins to 1968 with the formation of Association of International Bond Dealers (AIBD). The current ICMA, as we know it, was established in 2005. It is an independent body acting as a trade association for organisations operating in capital markets. ICMA's mission is to promote a well- functioning global debt security market, which in turn can establish sustainable economic development and growth *(Association,*

2021). Few of the ICMA established Bond standards are:

I. Green Bond Principles (GBP) – It is a set of guidelines establishing the voluntary process that recommends disclosure and transparency on the bond issuer's behalf. These guidelines provides the issuers for launching credible GBs, while also aiding the investors by promoting necessary information to evaluate the environmental impact of the bond investment. The guidelines also assist underwriters in facilitating transactions that further preserves the integrity of the GB market. GBP has established four core components - Use of proceeds, Process for Project Evaluation and Selection, Management of Proceeds and Reporting. They also recommend the need of external review for checking the alignment of GBs with the four core components. *(International Capital Market Association, 2021)*

II. Social Bond Principles (SBP) – Social bonds are type of bond instrument where proceeds are used for either financing or re-financing existing social projects. Like GBP, SBP are a set of guidelines for issuance of Social bonds. The defined eligible Social projects (but not limited to) are – Affordable basic structure (including potable water, sanitation, sewers, energy and transport), Access to essential services (like Healthcare, education, financial services etc.), Affordable housing, employment generation, food security and sustainable food systems and Socio-economic advancement and empowerment. The target population of Social bonds are people living under the poverty line, excluded or marginalised communities, persons with disabilities, displaced migrants, undereducated, unemployed, women, aging population or other vulnerable and marginalised populations and communities. The same four core components described in GBP segment apply over here as well. Although, SBP guidelines also establishes best practices in external review about second party opinion, Verification, Certification and Social bond Rating. *(International Capital Market Association, 2020)*

III. Sustainability-Linked Bond Principles (SLBP) – SLBPs refer to any type of bond instrument whose structural or financial characteristics can vary. The varying characteristics depend upon if the bond issuer achieves predetermined Environmental, social, and governance (ESG) or Sustainability objectives. In SLBPs the bond issuers commit themselves (in writing, in the documentation of the Bond) for a determined time in the future, to improve their sustainability outcomes. The key performance indicators determined by SLBPs are - Key Performance Indicators (KPIs) and Sustainability Performance Targets (SPTs). The SLBP guidelines has established five core components - Selection of Key Performance Indicators (KPIs), Calibration of Sustainability Performance Targets (SPTs), Bond characteristics, Reporting and Verification. *(International Capital Market Association, 2020)*

IV. Sustainability Bond Guidelines (SBG) – SBGs refer to any type of bond when the proceeds from the issuance is exclusively utilised for financing or refinancing a combination of both Social projects and Green projects. The SBGs four core components are the same to those laid by Social Bond Principles (SBPs) and Green Bond Principles (GBPs). Since often, Green projects have resultant social benefits and social projects might have certain green benefits; it is left on the part of bond issuer to classify the bond as Social bond, Sustainability bond or Green bond depending upon the project's primary objective. *(International Capital Market Association, 2021)*

The Climate Bond's Taxonomy Standard – Climate Bond Initiative is an international not-for-profit organisation working for investors. It has developed a bond standard along with certification, market intelligence and policy engagements. The Climate bond standard launched in December 2010 with the motive to help both the governments and the investor community. It identifies the infrastructure and developmental project needed for a low carbon economy by taking into account the global warming target set in the Paris agreement (of 2 Degree warming target) *(Bonds Initiative, 2021).* The standard specifically sets out guidelines for segments like energy, transport, water, buildings, land use & marine resources, industry, waste & pollution control and information & communication technology (ICT). The climate Bond standard follows a unique indicator system based on traffic light system where a green indication means 'automatically compatible', yellow indication means 'Compatible if compliant with screening indicator', red indication meaning 'not compatible' and a grey indication meaning 'more work required'. All these indicators are based solely upon whether or not the project adheres to the 2-Degree warming compliant norm set by the Paris agreement. *(Climate Bonds Initiative, 2021)*

ASEAN Green Bonds Standards – The ASEAN Green Bond standard makes it convenient for the capital markets of ASEAN countries to tap into the green finance sources. By doing so, it works for supporting sustainable growth and development of green finance sources for the region. The bond standards have been a result of collaboration with International Capital Market Association (ICMA). ICMA's Green Bond Principles (GBP) serves as the foundational pillar for the ASEAN Green Bond standard. The standard was introduced in November 2017 and has since been revised. For qualifying the GBs, as an 'ASEAN Green Bond' the issuer must be an ASEAN issuer; or the eligible green project must be located in any ASEAN country. The issuance of the GB must also originate from ASEAN member countries only. The set standards are very similar to earlier mentioned ICMA's GBPs with the only caveat being that it is meant to be used and issued in ASEAN member countries only. *(Forum, 2021)*

European Green Bond Standard – It was proposed on 6 July 2021. *(Jessop, 2021)* The standard aims to transform the EU's financial system more sustainable by creating a 'gold standard' of GBs, which can be compared with other set market standards. The proposed standard looks to establish inclusivity and will be open to all EU and non-EU issuers. The standard will be voluntary on the part of bond issuers with the set standard only applicable if they wish to market their bond offerings as 'European green bond'. Such bonds will used for financing projects up to 10 years. The first issuance under the standard is expected to undergo in 2021. *(Commission, 2021)*

These are some of the established and soon-to-be established Green Bonds Standards prevalent in use. With GBs becoming a major investment instrument, we can expect many more such standards to come up.

References

Association, I. (2021). The History of ICMA | About Us | ICMA. Icmagroup.org. Retrieved 8 September 2021, from https://www.icmagroup.org/About-ICMA/history/.

International Capital Market Association. (2021). Green Bond Principles Voluntary Process Guidelines for Issuing Green Bonds (pp. 1-10). ICMA. Retrieved from https://www.icmagroup.org/assets/documents/Sustainable-finance/2021-updates/Green-Bond-Principles-June-2021-140621.pdf

International Capital Market Association. (2020). Social Bond Principles Voluntary Process Guidelines for Issuing Social Bonds (pp. 1-8). International Capital Market Association. Retrieved from https://www.icmagroup.org/assets/documents/ Regulatory/Green-Bonds/June-2020/Social-Bond-PrinciplesJune-2020-090620.pdf

International Capital Market Association. (2020). Sustainability-Linked Bond Principles Voluntary Process Guidelines (pp. 1-11). International Capital Market Association. Retrieved from https://www.icmagroup.org/assets/documents/ Regulatory/Green-Bonds/June-2020/Sustainability-Linked-Bond-Principles-June-2020-171120.pdf

International Capital Market Association. (2021). Sustainability Bond Guidelines (pp. 1-5). International Capital Market Association. Retrieved from https://www.icmagroup.org/assets/documents/ Sustainable-finance/2021-updates/Sustainability-Bond-Guidelines-June-2021-140621.pdf

Bonds Initiative, C. (2021). History. Climate Bonds Initiative. Retrieved 8 September 2021, from https:// www.climatebonds.net/standard/about/history.

Climate Bonds Initiative. (2021). Climate Bonds Taxonomy. Climate Bonds Initiative. Retrieved from https://www.climatebonds.net/files/files/CBI_ Taxonomy_Tables-2June21.pdf

Forum, A. (2021). ASEAN Capital Markets Forum. Theacmf.org. Retrieved 8 September 2021, from https://www.theacmf.org/initiatives/sustainable-finance/asean-green-bond-standards.

Jessop, S. (2021). EU launches green bond framework to help it meet climate goals. Reuters. Retrieved 8 September 2021, from https://www.reuters.com/business/sustainable-business/eu-launches-green-bond-framework-help-it-meet-climate-goals-2021-07-06/.

Commission, E. (2021). European green bond standard. European Commission - European Commission. Retrieved 8 September 2021, from https://ec.europa.eu/info/business-economy-euro/banking-and-finance/sustainable-finance/european-green-bond-standard_en.

9

Different Sustainable Bond Labels

Necessity of Sustainable Bond Labels

Sustainable bond labels are specific tags, issued by a labelling agency. Such tags add transparency, credibility and better quality standards. Since common investor might find it difficult to make sense of various bond standards prevalent in the market, Sustainable fund labels can nudge them about the proposed bond's dedicated and responsible investment strategy. The Sustainable Bond label can vary according to the purpose like environmental, social and governance (ESG) Funds, Green funds or Social Funds. There are multiple Bond Labels established and available in each type of aforementioned bonds.

Some established ESG Sustainable Bond Labels

FNG Label - It is a label of Socially Responsible Investment (SRI) quality standard and used in German speaking countries. The label was established in 2015 after a development process of three years where key stakeholders were involved. The label certification provided by FNG must be annually renewed by the businesses. The fund label considers transparency, human and labour rights and environment protection as key areas. The applying company along with their products; is expected to have a clearly defined sustainability strategy. Businesses involved in coal mining, nuclear power generation, fracking, weapons and armaments are not eligible to apply for this label. The available ratings are based on criteria of "Institutional credibility", "Product Standards" and "Portfolio focus". There are four type of ratings - Basic, Mittel (1 star), Hoch (2 Star) and Sehr Hoch (3 Star). The Sehr Hoch rating is the highest available rating under FNG Seal. *(Siegel, 2021)*

Label ISR – Investissement Socialement Responsible (ISR) is a bond label created by France's Ministry of Economy & Finance in January 2016. It aims to let the investors distinguish between investment funds by implementing a robust methodology to measure the concrete results of Socially Responsible Investment (SRI). The Label has established a set of processes for funds applying for this label. These processes are – Defining the desired objective, Setting up an Analysis Methodology, Build and manage the Portfolio, Engage Stakeholders, Inform investors and Savers, and Evaluate the impact of the Approach. *(ISR, 2021)*

The four critical criteria the Label considers before giving the certification to any fund are –

- The environment (carbon footprint, greenhouse gas emissions, electricity consumption, water and waste management, etc.)
- Social (training of employees, equal pay for men and women, place of women in the management of the company, employment of disabled people, etc.)
- Governance (transparency on executive compensation, place of women on the board of directors, fight against corruption, etc.)
- Respect for human rights (fight against poverty, for example).

- *(ISR, 2021)*

LuxFLAG ESG – It is an ESG label from Luxembourg Finance Labelling Agency (LuxFLAG). LuxFLAG is a non-profit association formed in July 2006 when seven separate public and private founding partners (charter members) came together in Luxembourg. The LuxFLAG ESG label was itself launched in MAY 2014 as the first European ESG label. It is an international and independent labelling body, supporting mobilization of finances for development projects having sustainability as their core belief, while also bringing clarity to the potential investor. LuxFLAG is also a prominent part of Luxembourg fund industry (a community of over 1500 investment funds domiciled in Luxembourg). The core values of LuxFLAG is to embrace sustainability, transparency, independence and responsibility. The fund label is used for relevant projects in Microfinance, Green bonds, Environment, Climate finance and ESG. *(Luxflag, 2021)*

Nordic SWAN – It is an ecolabel established by Nordic Council of Ministers in 1989 as a voluntary Eco-labelling programme for the Nordic countries – Iceland, Sweden, Finland, Norway and Denmark. The ecolabel aims to reduce the environmental impact from production and consumption of goods by working in life cycle preservation, Circular economy and Green public procurement. The Nordic SWAN Ecolabel assess the entire life cycle of the product before issuing the certificate; right from raw material procurement stage to production, consumption, disposal and recycling. The certificate is offered in 59 different product groups with more than 200 different product types. The Nordic SWAN ecolabel also has the distinction to be one of the founders of Global Ecolabelling Network in 1994. *(Swan, 2021)*

Österreichisches Umweltzeichen – It is the state-certified environmental seal in Austria founded in 1990 and headquartered in Vienna. The ecolabel is provided for products such as building & living, household & cleaning, office products, garden & outdoors, green energy, sustainable finance, Mobility, shoes & textile and Film production. The Ecolabel was introduced in 1996 for tourism businesses, ecolabel for the education sector in 2002 and eco-label for Green Meetings & Green Events in 2010. Industry specific technical committees develop the guidelines for the ecolabel; "Environmental Label Advisory Board", an advisory Committee of the Ministry of the Environment, then scrutinizes the recommendations made by the committee. The policies are then decided which are vendor-independent and practice-oriented. *(Umweltzeichen, 2021)*

Greenfin Label – This label was created by Ministry of Ecological Transition, France. The label guarantees the green quality of investment funds and is aimed at financial actors who act in the service of the common good through transparent and sustainable practices. The label has the particularity of excluding funds that invest in companies operating in the nuclear sector and fossil fuels. It was the first state label dedicated to green finance, the Greenfin label (formerly the "Energy and ecological transition for the climate" label) was launched at the end of 2015. The public authorities own the label (brand, regulations of use, reference system) and approve the label development proposals made by the Greenfin label committee. The Greenfin label committee defines the broad guidelines for coordinating the entire system and proposes changes to the label specifications to the public authorities. The funds applying for the label must ensure active monitoring of environmental (E), social (S) and governance (G) controversies, and demonstrate their impact on the construction and life of the portfolio. The Greenfin label granted for a period of one year after which it is due for Renewal. During the one-year period, intermediate checks are scheduled to verify that the fund complies with the requirements of the label. *(Greenfin, 2021)*

GreenPro – GreenPro is an Ecolabel from India, which was formed by Confederation of Indian Industry (CII) in January 2018. The ecolabel has a three-pronged agenda of - increasing the demand of Green products in the market, enabling the end consumers with right knowledge to choose better green products and equipment, and to make a system following which a product can be recognised as 'Green'. The GreenPro ecolabel follows a life cycle approach where it evaluates the products based on – Raw materials, manufacturing process, product's performance during use, disposal or recycling, and associated benefits. The ecolabel also aims to address the national priorities of water conservation, land conservation, energy efficiency and renewable energy production. The certification marks the products in 'Credit Points'. The maximum achievable points are 100 while, anf product achieving 50 or more points is certified 'Green Product'. The validity of the certification is of 2 years after which the manufacturers are expected to renew the GreenPro certification. *(Greenpro, 2021)*

The Global Ecolabelling Network (GEN) – GEN is an internationally recognised platform having many Eco-labelling organisations registered under it. It was founded in 1994 with the aim to conserve environment while also promoting the need to do so. It also promotes development of ecolabels for green products and even sustainable services. There are 33 full members, associate members and affiliate members of GEN spread across the globe. While GEN itself doesn't develops the criterias certifying any product as 'Green'; it supports its members to do so by developing ecolabels and other regulations. *(Network, 2021)*

Below mentioned is the full member list of GEN:

Country	Programme Name	Organisation
Australia	Good Environmental Choice Australia	Good Environmental Choice Australia
Brazil	ABNT Ecolabel - Hummingbird	Associação Brasileira de Normas Técnicas
China (CEC)	China Environmental Labelling	China Environmental United Certification Center
China (CQC)	China Environmentally Friendly Certification	China Quality Certification Centre (CQC)
Chinese Taipei	Green Mark Program	Environment and Development Foundation
European Union	EU Ecolabel	European Commission
Germany	The Blue Angel Eco-Label	German Federal Environment Agency
Germany (TUV)	Green Product Mark	TÜV Rheinland

Hong Kong (GC)	Hong Kong Green Label Scheme	Green Council
India	GreenPro	Confederation of Indian Industry
Indonesia	Indonesian Ecolabel	Ministry of Environment
Israel	Israeli Green Label	The Standards Institution of Israel
Japan	Eco Mark Program	Japan Environment Association (JEA)
Kazakhstan	Eco-Labelling	International Academy of Ecology of the Republic of Kazakhstan
Korea	Korean Eco-Label Program	KEITI (Korea Environmental Industry and Technology Institute)
Malaysia	SIRIM Eco-Labelling Scheme	SIRIM QAS International Sdn Bhd

New Zealand	Environmental Choice New Zealand	The New Zealand Ecolabelling Trust
Nordic Countries	Nordic Swan Ecolabel	Nordic Ecolabelling Board
North America	ECOLOGO	UL Environment
Philippines	Green Choice Philippines	Philippine Center for Environmental Protection and Sustainable Development (PCEPSD)
Russia	Vitality Leaf	Ecological Union
Singapore	Singapore Green Labelling Scheme	Singapore Environment Council
Sweden (SSNC)	Good Environmental Choice	The Swedish Society for Nature Conservation
Sweden	TCO Certified	TCO Development
Thailand	Green Label: Thailand	Thailand Environment Institute

| Ukraine | Green Crane | All Ukrainian NGO Living Planet |
| United States | Green Seal | Green Seal Inc. |

(Network, 2021)

Note – It is not mandatory for an Eco-Label to be a part of The Global Ecolabelling Network (GEN). Many Eco-labels function independently or according to their parent government or regularizing body. For e.g. Luxembourg's LuxFlag, Austria's Österreichisches Umweltzeichen, Canada's EnerGuide label etc.

References

Siegel, F. (2021). Einführung – FNG-Siegel. Fng-siegel.org. Retrieved 8 September 2021, from https://fng-siegel.org/einfuehrung/.

ISR, L. (2021). Label ISR. Label ISR. Retrieved 8 September 2021, from https://www.lelabelisr.fr/.

Luxflag, L. (2021). Who we are. Luxflag.org. Retrieved 8 September 2021, from https://www.luxflag.org/about/who-we-are.html.

Swan, N. (2021). The official ecolabel of the Nordic countries. Nordic Ecolabel. Retrieved 8 September

2021, from https://www.nordic-ecolabel.org/the-nordic-swan-ecolabel/.

Umweltzeichen, Ö. (2021). Sustainable Finance ← Products ← Umweltzeichen.at. Umweltzeichen. at. Retrieved 8 September 2021, from https://www. umweltzeichen.at/en/products/sustainable-finance.

Greenfin, L. (2021). Le label Greenfin. Ministère de la Transition écologique. Retrieved 15 April 2021, from https://www.ecologie.gouv.fr/label-greenfin.

Greenpro, G. (2021). Greenpro | Home. Ciigreenpro. com. Retrieved 8 September 2021, from https:// www.ciigreenpro.com/about.

Network, G. (2021). Internationally recognised ecolabelling orgs | Global Ecolabelling Network. Globalecolabelling.net. Retrieved 8 September 2021, from https://globalecolabelling.net/about/gen-the-global-ecolabelling-network/.

Network, G. (2021). Green companies, organisations & government bodies | Global Ecolabelling Network. Globalecolabelling.net. Retrieved 8 September 2021, from https://globalecolabelling.net/gen-members/gen-full-members-list/.

10

Sustainable Bond Issuing Process

The Sustainable Bond issuing process may vary slightly from one country to another given the requirements of various legal nature. However, the basic process of issuing a sustainable bond remains the same. *(Climate Bonds Initiative, 2021)* The whole process can be divided into 3 Segments:

1. Pre-Issuance
2. Issuance
3. Post-Issuance

Pre-Issuance

This step is concerned with defining a Sustainable bond framework for the bond. The bond issuers draft a detailed document detailing out the projects and sub-projects, which will be financed from the proceeds of the sustainable bond. The document will also give plans for management of proceeds along with the commitment of the issuer for reporting the developments in a timely manner.

It is in this step that the issuer can refer to any Sustainable bond standards and labels (described in previously chapters) which they are aligning with. They will also have to reveal the broad category for eligible sustainable project for e.g. – Renewable energy, Green Building, Clean transportation, Waste management etc. The issuer will also explicitly mention about the bond's sustainability objective, along with the process to be adhered for project evaluation. The internal process used for selection and approval of the project will also have to be documented.

The issuer will need to disclose about reconciliation done periodically until the bond remains outstanding giving out details of project expenditure and unallocated balance. The auditing organisation to be deployed for verifying the allocation process can also be revealed at this point. The method and timeline of reporting will also be mentioned for allocation of proceeds followed by annual reporting practices to increase transparency and investor confidence. The sustainability project must have an external review along with a Second party opinion from auditing/ consulting firms giving Verification, Certification and Ratings to the Sustainable bond. *(Climate Bonds Initiative, 2021)*

Issuance

Once the bond is structured, it may be issued by either:

- ☐ Making an offer to the Public
- ☐ By making Preferential offer

i. Making an offer to the Public

In such a case, the issuer will circulate a Prospectus as per the legal requirements of the country it is offering the Bond along with all the prerequisite steps to be followed by the applicants in order to make themselves eligible for subscribing the bond.

ii. By making Preferential offer

The preferential offer can be a private placement meant for institutional investors. The offer will have to be approved by the law and will have to state all the requirements on the part of both issuer and the buying corporation for buying and subsequent repayment process. *(Climate Bonds Initiative, 2021)*

Post-Issuance

Under the Post-Issuance stage, the bond issuer reports about the Allocation of Proceeds by detailing out the allocation for each project on a periodical basis. The timeline to be adhered at this stage is as per the announcement made at the Pre-Issuance stage and in line with Bond framework. The issuer may also report the perceived impact of the bond using key performance indicator (KPI). This step of the Bond issuance is particularly important as it provides the confirmation and comfort to the investors subscribed to the bond. The issuer may also, from time to time, adhere to Anti Money Laundering (AML) compliance of the country to ensure that the Bond instrument is not misused.

In case of some unallocated funds from the proceeds remaining, the issuer should also disclose whether the same have been held in some temporary investment instrument. It is noteworthy, that any such temporary parking of funds must also comply with sustainability factor and should not be parked in any way to benefit some greenhouse intensive or other fossil fuel depending project.

This stage is also responsible for properly monitoring a project and publish timely reports of Audits and second party reviews. *(Climate Bonds Initiative, 2021)*

Types of Possible Bond Labels

Although, in the book we have discussed about Sustainable and Green Bonds, it is imperative to note that there can be many possible bond labels identifying themselves differently while working for sustainability. The possible Bond labels have been listed below.

Bond Label	First Issuance Year	Eligible Project Uses
Blue Bonds	2018	Protection of Marine Habitat, Sustainable Practices of Fishing
Disaster/ Catastrophe Bonds	2014	Supports governments in rehabilitation efforts after any climate disasters.
Climate Action Bonds	2019	Sustainable development and Energy transition projects
Climate Awareness Bonds	2007	Energy Efficiency and Renewable Energy Projects

Climate Bonds	2010	Sustainable Use of Land, Water Resources Conservation and Renewable Energy
Climate Resilience Bond	2019	Development of Infrastructure (such as water, Clean Energy, Clean transportation and other similiar urban infrastructure); Agriculture & Ecological systems.
Development Impact Bonds	2018	Education for Girls
ESG Bonds	2019	Projects is line with Environmental, Social and Governance Sustainability principles
Environmental Bonds	2019	Energy Efficiency including Renewable Energy Projects; Green Buildings and Clean Transportation
Environmental Sustainability Bonds	2010	Sustainable Resource Projects (such as Water conservation, Energy conservation and Pollution Prevention), Climate Projects

Forest Bonds	2016	Works for Projects in Forest Conservation and promoting Afforestation
Green Bonds	2010	Green projects on Sustainable Use of Land, Water Conservation, Renewable Energy production and other such initiatives
Green Convertible Bonds	2020	Primarily for Financing and refinancing of Projects based upon Renewable energy production (solar, or wind power) or Energy storage activities
Green Contingent Convertible Bonds	2020	Primarily for projects working for energy efficiency, renewable energy production, sustainable and clean transportation, water conservation and waste management
Green Transition Bonds	2019	For building Infrastructure, food production or green buildings

Pandemic Bonds	2017	For projects working against spread of infectious diseases and its containment
SDG Bonds	2020	For Projects working in Environmental Preservation and climate sensitive fields such as Affordable housing and Renewable energy
Social Bonds	2017	Working for Marginalized populations in emerging countries, promoting inclusion of women and low-income communities having limited access to basic infrastructure, finance and other basic facilities
Social Impact Bonds	2010	Programs for social welfare with the aim of bringing benefits to local beneficiaries and regional govt.

Social Inclusion Bonds	2017	Programs Supporting MSMEs to strengthen job creation and preservation; Community housing for marginalised and vulnerable population groups; also working for their vocational training and education.
Sustainability (Awareness) Bonds	2018	Projects working in developing countries improving Water Quality, promoting Access to Sanitation and other such infrastructure projects
Sustainable Transition Bonds	2019	Projects working for Improving the environmental and social standards of supply chains
Sustainable Development Bonds	2017	Projects working for promoting - Sustainable Cities, Gender Equality, building Climate Resilience, and protecting Marine and Water Resources76543

Sustainable Growth Bonds	2017	Projects working in the area of Sustainable Cities Gender Equality, building Climatic Resilience and Conserving Marine and Water Resources
Transition/	2017	For projects working in the area of Climate related transition activities

(Schumacher, 2020)

References

Climate Bonds Initiative. (2021). How to Issue Green Bonds, Social Bonds and Sustainability Bonds (pp. 19-24). Climate Bonds Initiative. Retrieved from https://asianbondsonline.adb.org/green-bonds/pdf/How%20to%20Issue%20Guide%20English%20FINAL%20PRINT.pdf

Schumacher, D. (2020). Green Bonds: The Shape of Green Fixed-Income Investing to Come. The Journal Of Environmental Investing, 10(1), 7-15. Retrieved 8 September 2021, from https://www.thejei.com/wp-content/uploads/2020/08/Complete-JEI-Vol.-10-no-1-2020.pdf.

11

Regulatory Framework of Green Bonds in India

Green debt securities are similar to other debt instruments issued for the aim of obtaining capital. Green debt securities are unique from conventional bonds since the funds raised must be used for environmentally friendly business ventures and product offerings. Also, it has stringent requirements regarding project evaluation and its selection; along with management of proceeds and subsequent reporting.

Companies in India can issue both unlisted and listed green debt securities. While there are no special standards for unlisted green debt securities beyond the normal requirements for debt securities issuance, issuances of listed green debt securities must adhere to the following regulations:

- SEBI Regulations 2021 (Non-Convertible Securities Regulations);
- The SEBI Regulations, 2015 (Listing Obligations and Disclosure Requirements Regulations); and
- The Chapter IX SEBI Operational Circular for Non-Convertible Securities Issue and Listing.

Use of Proceeds Requirements

Under the Disclosure requirements for issuance and listing green bonds, it has been specifically mentioned that for designating the bonds as Green, the main categories of investments in which such funds may be invested in the following areas:

- Energy that is renewable and sustainable (wind, solar etc.)
- Transportation that is environmentally friendly (mass transportation)
- Water management that is sustainable (clean and/or drinking water, water recycling, etc.)

☐ Adaptation to climate change

☐ Efficient energy use (efficient and green buildings)

☐ Waste management that is sustainable (recycling, waste to energy etc.)

☐ Land use that is sustainable (includes sustainable forestry and agriculture, as well as afforestation)

☐ Conservation of biological variety, or

☐ Any other category that SEBI may specify from time to time.

☐ ("Disclosure Requirements for Issuance and Listing Green Bonds", 2022)

Disclosures to be made in case of Issuing Green Debt Securities

1. A statement outlining the environmental aims of the Green Debt Securities offering

2. Brief description of the decision-making process used by the issuer to determine the eligibility of the project(s) and/or asset(s) for which proceeds from the issuance of Green Debt Securities are to be raised. The following is a general outline of the information that should be provided:

    a. The procedure followed/to be followed in establishing how the project(s)and/or asset(s) falls within the stated categories of qualified green projects

b. The criteria for eligibility of the project(s) and/or asset(s) to receive revenues from Green Debt Securities; and

c. Environmental and long-term sustainability goals of the proposed green investment.

3. The issuer shall specify the system/procedures that will be used to track the distribution of the issue's proceeds.

4. The project(s) and/or asset(s) or locations for which the issuer intends to use the proceeds of the Green Debt Securities, including any existing green project(s) and/or asset(s), if any.

5. The issuer may engage an independent third-party reviewer/certifier to review/certify the issuer's processes, which may include project evaluation and selection criteria, project categories suitable for financing through Green Debt Securities, and so forth. Appointing a reviewer/certifier is optional and at the issuer's discretion; nevertheless, any such appointment shall be stated in the offer document.

6. ("Disclosure Requirements for Issuance and Listing Green Bonds", 2022)

SEBI Prescribed other Requirements

Apart from the above points, the SEBI Operational Circular imposes various duties on issuers of Green Debt Securities. Not only should projects financed with revenues from Green Debt Securities meet the eligibility criteria, but they should also maintain that eligibility throughout their life cycle, while also meeting the environmental objectives indicated in the offer document. The issuers must maintain a decision-making process to ensure such continuity and compliance with the proceeds utilisation.

Continuous disclosure requirements

Along with the half-year and annual financial results, the issuer who has listed its Green Debt Securities will publish the Utilization of the offering proceeds in accordance with the tracking conducted by the issuer in line with the specific mechanism specified in the offer document/disclosure document. The proceeds shall be validated through an external auditor's report, which will verify the internal tracking system and the allocation of cash from the proceeds of Green Debt Securities to the project(s) and/or asset(s). Apart from this, it will also provide details of any unutilised proceeds.

Additional disclosures, which must be included with the yearly report, are:

☐ A list of the project(s) and/or asset(s) to which revenues from the Green Debt Securities were allocated/invested, together with a brief description of the project(s) and/or asset(s) and the amounts disbursed. Where confidentiality agreements restrict the amount of detail that can be disclosed regarding specific projects and/or assets, information about the areas in which such projects and/or assets fall shall be supplied.

☐   Qualitative performance indicators and, if possible, quantitative performance metrics of the project(s) and/or asset's environmental impact (s). If the quantitative benefits/impact on the environment cannot be determined, the fact may be stated appropriately along with the reasons for the inability to determine the benefits/impact on the environment.

☐   The methods and underlying assumptions that were utilised to develop the performance indicators and metrics.

("SEBI | Disclosure Requirements for Issuance and Listing of Green Debt Securities", 2017)

References

Disclosure Requirements for Issuance and Listing Green Bonds. (2022). Retrieved 11 January 2022, from https://www.sebi.gov.in/sebi_data/meetingfiles/1453349548574-a.pdf

SEBI | Disclosure Requirements for Issuance and Listing of Green Debt Securities. (2017). Retrieved 11 January 2022, from https://www.

sebi.gov.in/legal/circulars/may-2017/disclosure-requirements-for-issuance-and-listing-of-green-debt-securities_34988.html

Conclusion

Industries in India are largely funded by banks and non-banking financial institutions. In order to avoid an asset-liability mismatch, these institutions are reluctant to provide long-term financing for renewable energy projects. To enable capacity expansion that is financially less rewarding in the short run, but nonetheless very important for the sustainability of the environment, existing traditional financing sources are insufficient and exploration of new funding opportunities is the need of the hour.

Green Bonds will address the financial issues that generally delay renewable energy project development. Bonds issued to fund renewable energy initiatives must only be issued by companies that invest in renewable energy, waste management, clean transportation, and sustainable land use.

By 2022, India looks forward to building 175 GW of renewable energy capacity, up from 30 GW now. This herculean task will need funds in excess of $200 billion. It's particularly hard given the fact that traditional financing options won't consider this "financially less lucrative" investing option. In India, funding and long-term expense sustainability have been major roadblocks in such "green" initiatives.

Green Bonds help issuers diversify funding and reduce market reliance. Green bonds are particularly popular among ESG and sustainable and ethical investors (Environmental, Social, and Governance). The money is raised for specific green initiatives. The issuer, not the investor, carries the risk of failure. Green bonds also help renewable energy by lowering interest rates and extending payback times.

In 2015, India was one of the top issuers of green bonds. In the third quarter of 2017, India issued $1.95 billion in green bonds, ranking fifth globally. We can say that green bonds are gaining popularity in India.

It has increased capital inflow from global investors and access to funding at various stages of the project lifecycle. This commitment to sustainability also helps the issuer's reputation and enhances the firm's goodwill. Renewable energy, thus, is a key sector for such "green" investment.

It was in 2015 that SEBI approved the Green Bond standards in India. SEBI's support for green bonds is significant as it also issued Green Bond Guidelines, which codify the issuance of green bonds and provide investor reassurance. Its assistance delivered to finance India's rapidly increasing sustainable energy business is noteworthy. Making green bonds more accessible to investors helps the renewable energy sector. They should assist investors by focusing on green initiatives and maintaining transparency. Indian initiatives are drawing foreign investment as the global green bond market expands rapidly.

Although, just regulations are not enough to keep green bonds afloat in India. Regulators can start the market, but investors must sustain it. Currently, conventional investors buy green bonds based on credit fundamentals rather than green criteria. Clearly, more investors would need to buy green bonds. Only time will tell how green bonds may shape India's sustainability commitments in the future.

www.ingramcontent.com/pod-product-compliance
Lightning Source LLC
LaVergne TN
LVHW051446170726
843492LV00002B/572